For my wonderful Grandpa

First published in Great Britain in 2021

Text Copyright Molly Copestake 2021
Illustration Copyright Alex Crump 2021

All rights reserved
ISBN 978-1-8383415-8-9

Molly Copestake asserts the moral right to be identified as the author of the work.

Alex Crump asserts the moral right to be identified as the illustrator of the work.

Conditions of Sale

Mr Pippety Poppety's Birthday

By Molly Copestake

Illustrated by Alex Crump

Deep in the trunks of Oak Tree Wood there lived a little man named Mr Pippety Poppety. But Mr Pippety Poppety was no ordinary man. Oh no, he was a teeny tiny man no bigger than your finger who could squeeze and squash his way through the tiny gap in the trunk of the big oak tree that led to his home.

The front entrance was about the size of an oak leaf and inside was pretty tiny too. His bowls were made from small acorn shells and his table was crafted from trimmings from a log with four little sticks holding it up.

2

He ate porridge with juicy forest berries for breakfast, cheese and ham sandwiches for lunch and jelly and ice cream for tea, *yum, yum, fill my tum.*

Up the wobbly wooden stairs it was just as homely and cosy. He had placed a leafy red rug that spread gloriously over the middle of the room like a red river of jelly flooding the bedroom.

Over to the corner of the room was a comfy red bed with a knitted blanket to keep the miniature man toasty and warm as the cold winters approached.

Mr Pippety Poppety had his favourite picture hanging on the wall above his bed. It was of him, Mr Badger and Mr Hedgehog all tucking into a big bowl of jelly and ice cream. *Yum, yum, fill my tum!*

This was from Mr Pippety Poppety's last birthday. They had dancing, eating and lots of fun!

Mr Badger and Mr Hedgehog were Mr Pippety Poppety's best friends in the whole wide world. They both lived next door to him, and they always had so much fun together. But their favourite thing to do together was to eat… jelly and ice cream, *yum, yum, fill my tum!* Mr Pippety Poppety loved it more than anything else in the world and ate it for tea every day. Imagine that!

Our story begins one autumn day. Mr Pippety Poppety was very excited indeed. Tomorrow was going to be his birthday! He couldn't wait. All of his friends in Oak Tree Wood were coming to his party. His best friends Mr Badger and Mr Hedgehog were coming and all of his other friends too.

There was timid Mrs Rabbit and Mr Rabbit who lived opposite him, brave Mr Robin who lived above him and Mrs Squirrel with her squealing squirrel twins, Sophie and Sammy Squirrel, who lived above the rabbit family.

Mr Pippety Poppety was particularly excited this year as he had booked a magician to come and do magic tricks and entertain his friends.

Mr Pippety Poppety had prepared a picnic tea for everyone to enjoy and munch on to make his birthday party even better.

His party guests would all be bringing gifts for him and as usual they would play lots of fun games like pass the parcel and musical statues. He couldn't wait for the fun to begin!

When he went to bed that night, Mr Pippety Poppety heard the phone ring. The poor man nearly jumped out of his skin!

He picked up the phone cautiously. Mr Pippety Poppety rarely got calls, as all of his friends lived with him in Oak Tree Wood.

'Hello,' said the man on the phone, 'is that Mr Pippety Poppety? It's Mr Abra K Dabra here.'

'Yes this is Mr Pippety Poppety. I'm looking forward to you performing at my birthday party tomorrow,' replied Mr Pippety Poppety. 'I'm so excited about it!'

'Er… well that's why I'm calling. I'm truly sorry but I have to cancel. I've double booked myself!' Mr Abra K Dabra said awkwardly, 'I am truly sorry.' Then he quickly hung up.

Mr Pippety Poppety felt very sad indeed. His birthday party wouldn't be the same without a magician. What was he going to do?

That night he dreamt about his party. He imagined it to be a total disaster. He dreamt his friends were so disappointed that they all left the party and decided that they didn't even want to be his friends anymore. They moved away from him, away from Oak Tree Wood, to live a new life, all because of his failed birthday party.

When he woke up, he realised this would never happen, but it still worried him.

Mr Pippety Poppety tried to make himself feel better by treating himself to a bowl of delicious ice cream for a birthday breakfast treat.

Yum, yum, fill my tum!

He planned to eat jelly for lunch. Maybe it would be a great day after all.

But as time edged closer and closer to the party, he became more and more worried.

When it was only ten minutes until his guests were due to arrive, he decided there was only one thing for it. He had to find another magician and make his birthday party extra special again.

Mr Pippety Poppety strolled outside to clear his head and have a think. He walked to the edge of the woods and stared out at the town where all the giant humans lived.

But then, he heard a loud ka-thump, ka-thump, ka-THUMP which seemed to be coming towards him!

Three gigantic giants had stomped into the otherwise peaceful woodlands.

All the animals hiding in their tree trunks were shaking with fear. But not Mr Pippety Poppety!

He had never seen humans before but he had heard that they were big, scary beasts that stomped and stamped and shouted and peered until they had scared the creatures straight out of their homes.

But what Mr Pippety Poppety saw didn't look scary or stompy. These giants looked happy and chatty skipping along together.

So he decided it would be polite to go and say hello. The tiny man walked right up to the giant humans and yelled at the top of his voice, 'Hello kind giants!'

They all stopped and looked around.

'Did you hear that, Grandpa?' asked the smallest of the giants, curiously. 'It sounded like… a tiny man!'

'Don't be so silly Oscar!' laughed the middle-sized giant. 'What is it Grandpa?' but the giant she was talking to, the tallest of all three, wasn't listening. He was stroking his chin and staring at Mr Pippety Poppety in disbelief.

'Hello,' he said softly, 'how are you today?' He turned to his grandchildren. 'Hey, you two. Come and meet this little man over here.'

'I'm not too good. It's my birthday, you see, but my entertainment has been cancelled, and now everything will be ruined!' moaned Mr Pippety Poppety.

'Oh dear. Can I help in any way?' the man inquired.

The middle-sized giant, a kindly looking creature added 'My name is Molly, and this,' she pointed at the smallest giant, 'is my brother Oscar.'

'Also, this is my Grandpa but we call him Magic Grandpa, because he's a magician!' Oscar said, referring to the tallest giant.

'Really? Well wobble my jelly! I need a magician for my party. Would you consider performing?' he asked politely. 'I'm Mr Pippety Poppety by the way.'

'I would love to!' Magic Grandpa laughed.

'But I'm expecting my guests really soon. You haven't had any time to prepare!' panicked Mr Pippety Poppety.

'I think we'll be fine.' the giant smiled.

'You said we…' started Oscar.

'Does that mean…' wondered Molly excitedly.

'You two can help me if you like?' Magic Grandpa said cheerfully.

'Yay!' shouted the pair, jumping for joy.

Whilst Magic Grandpa practised his tricks, Mr Pippety Poppety marched confidently down to the golden willow tree, where his friends would be gathering for the party. Everyone in the woods had been to parties there, but none of them had ever been to one with three giant magicians! But when he stepped into the mossy green clearing there was no one there. Just a few soft mushrooms coloured ruby red, sunshine yellow and pumpkin orange.

A blue and white striped picnic rug was spread across the grass for the friends to sit on while they watched the magic show. But there would be no magic show or indeed any party if nobody showed up. He felt his spirits drop and he started to panic. What if they had found out about his missing magician cancelling and decided they wouldn't be friends with him anymore? What if his nightmare came true?

Mr Pippety Poppety felt like crying. Suddenly, he heard a little giggle from under a mushroom and an angry 'shh' from another. He didn't know which was worse, thinking that all his friends had skipped his birthday party or that there was something very scary waiting to jump out at him!

Who was under that mushroom? Was it a ghost? Or maybe… a super scary, petrifying, terribly spooky woodcutter! He didn't know much about these beasts and had never seen one but he was told that they were horrid creatures that destroyed people's homes and invaded their forest. He did not want to run into one of those!

But just as he was about to investigate further, his friends leaped out from under the table and yelled, 'We're here!'

Mr Pippety Poppety was so happy that his party guests had shown up. Everyone had a lovely party and played fun party games until they were tired and needed a little sit down.

It was time for Mr Pippety Poppety to surprise them. The magic show would start any minute. He couldn't wait. He knew his new friends wouldn't disappoint him. All the party guests crowded round and sat on the picnic rug waiting for the show to start.

When Magic Grandpa stepped out and introduced himself, there was a slight gasp as humans aren't normally seen in Oak Tree Wood. But when they realised he was friendly they soon calmed down. The sun shone on his head like a spotlight whilst everyone cheered and Molly and Oscar prepared the first trick.

'Today I have two tricks to show you.' Magic Grandpa announced. The audience cooed happily. 'Now let's start the first trick. As you can see, I am very clearly a giant to you. But if I'm going to show you all magic tricks I'll have to be your size, right?' Everyone nodded approvingly. 'Well then, have a look inside this rainbow bag.'

All the tiny animals took turns to look into the giant bag. They were very good at sharing and when they had all had a turn Sophie Squirrel announced that there were three orange sweets sitting in the bottom of the glittery pouch.

Magic Grandpa pulled one of the sweets out and told the audience, 'What you see here looks like an ordinary sweet. But there is a lot more to this sugary treat. It will do something truly magical to anyone who lets it enter their mouths. So, should I eat it?'

'Yes!' they all shouted. So he swallowed the orange sweet and as the sugary flavours overwhelmed his mouth he began to shrink.

Down, down, down he went until he was the exact same size as all the party guests and birthday boy! Everyone clapped and cheered. Once they'd stopped, Magic Grandpa declared, 'I will now do the same to my assistants, Magnificent Molly and Outstanding Oscar!'

The friends in the audience cheered excitedly and were enjoying themselves so much they were practically jumping up and down. So Molly and Oscar looked at each other nervously and then swallowed the carrot-coloured candy and they too began to shrink down, down, down until they were both the size of Mr Pippety Poppety.

Everyone cheered and clapped, still stunned by the extraordinary trick.

'Surely,' thought Mr Pippety Poppety, 'that has to be the best magic I've ever seen!'

'For my second trick today,' Magic Grandpa announced, 'we will be using this shiny silver tin.' He showed the audience. 'You see,' he whispered mysteriously, 'there is nothing in it. Please can I have a volunteer? You at the back, what's your name?'

He was pointing at Mrs Rabbit. She blushed and muttered quietly, 'My name is Mrs Rabbit!'

'Wonderful,' said Magic Grandpa, 'please hop to the front.'

Mrs Rabbit jumped nervously up to Magic Grandpa and asked him, 'Is it dangerous?' But he just chuckled reassuringly and smiled at her.

'Please look inside the tin. Feel free to peer around.'

The tin was still human sized and so Mrs Rabbit had to jump inside to see!

It looked very funny as she was peering around with a hilarious expression on her face. 'Nothing down here!' she yelled. Mrs Rabbit climbed out and was asked to take a bow. Once she had done so, she hopped back into the audience, smiling happily.

'Now,' smiled Magic Grandpa, 'we have to make a special birthday surprise. Who wants to help? I'll have the birthday boy, and you two at the back,' he said pointing at Mr Badger and Sammy Squirrel. 'Now Mr Pippety Poppety, please follow this recipe and put in the first ingredient.'

Magic Grandpa had arranged a line of strange things on a small, oak table. Mr Pippety Poppety read the recipe. It was very silly! The first ingredient was an orange rubber lizard! Mr Pippety Poppety dropped in the giant lizard and sat back down.

Next, Mr Badger read the second ingredient, which was a sprinkle of magic dust. So that's just what he put in.

Finally, little Sammy Squirrel sprayed a squirt of golden unicorn's tears into the mixture.

Magic Grandpa stirred the strange ingredients round and round in the glistening tin. He replaced the lid, then he whispered a special magic word, 'Abracadabra' and tapped it with his black and white magic wand.

When he carefully lifted the lid, inside were nine glorious golden cakes, each iced with swirly buttercream and topped with rainbow sprinkles!

All the guests jumped for joy and each munched on a cupcake saying they were incredible and so was the trick. Mr Pippety Poppety felt so lucky.

Once they had each munched on their treats, it was time for tea. With all the chaos about the magic show, Mr Pippety Poppety had forgotten to bring the party food! But when his friends brought out a surprise party tea he was overjoyed! There was jelly that wobbled so high it nearly hit the branches on the tree and scoops of ice cream so large they had to be scooped out by a digger.

He jumped around yelling, *'Yum, yum, fill my tum!'* over and over again.

They all tucked in and Magic Grandpa took a brilliant photo of all the guests singing Happy Birthday.

When Mr Pippety Poppety cut the jelly, he wished
that all his birthdays could be as special as this one.

The End.

About the Author

My name is Molly Copestake and I am 10 years old. I live in Swindon with my Mum, Dad and younger brothers Oscar and Sam. I have always loved writing stories and dreamt of being an author.

When I was little my Grandpa used to tell me stories about a tiny man that lives in the woods. Every time we went on a walk he would take him out of his pocket and make up a story about his adventures.

My Grandpa is also a magician and used to perform magic tricks for us whenever we saw him and at my birthday parties. As I got older I became his helper. I really hope you enjoyed reading my story.

A note from Magic Grandpa:

Hello. I am Molly's Grandpa – Magic Grandpa in fact! I thought you might like to know about the background to Mr Pippety Poppety.

Many years ago when my three daughters were young, we lived near some woods and used to walk there frequently. I don't remember why, but on one walk I decided to pretend I had seen a small door at the base of a tree trunk. I went towards it, called the girls over and they 'saw' the door. We knocked and out came my imaginary character Mr Pippety Poppety. I held him in the palm of my hand, they also 'saw' him and we chatted and from that moment on, I have told literally hundreds of Mr Pippety Poppety stories to my three girls and now to my grandchildren. Every time we met they asked for stories. He accompanied us on walks, holidays and journeys, and we have 'travelled' into outer space, gone deep underground – you name it we've been there.

As a primary school headteacher, I would go into classes, produce him from my pocket and hand him round the circle of children and never once did any child not 'see' him.

I have always been amazed how children have accepted this imaginary character along with Mr Badger and Mr Hedgehog. I have no recollection of why I chose those names or animals – all I do know is they have been a hit with all children.

As a hobby, I was also a children's magician and performed the cake trick used in the story at Molly and her brother Oscar's birthday parties.

In March 2020 I was diagnosed with Motor Neurone Disease, and by June had lost the use of my voice, so the stories have ceased... until now! I am so proud of Molly because she promised me that she would carry on telling the stories to her younger brothers and her younger cousins. And then this story appeared!

I hope you enjoyed reading about Mr Pippety Poppety. When you are next out for a walk maybe see if you can find him. He might be hiding in his house among the trees or you might even find him in someone's pocket. Have a look now, see if he is there!

David Ellis

29th July 1953 - 1st August 2021

Printed in Great Britain
by Amazon

66715758R00024